Little Sammy's Big Trip

CRISTI ROPP

NEWMAN SPRINGS PUBLISHING
320 Broad Street
Red Bank, NJ 07701

First originally published by Newman Springs Publishing 2021

ISBN 978-1-64096-193-7 (Paperback)
ISBN 978-1-64096-194-4 (Digital)

Printed in the United States of America

To my daughter whom I was expecting when the original script was written and who always believed in my dreams.

On one bright and sunny day,
Sammy Squirrel went out to play.
He saw some hay piled in a truck
and thought, *Oh! What good luck.*

Forgetting what his mother did say,
he climbed in to roll in the hay.

While he was romping in the heap,
he got tired and fell asleep.

When he awoke, he was far from home.

Because the truck began to roam.

Then the truck came to a stop,

and Sammy poked his head over the top.

The farmer opened his door and got out,

and he began to look about.

Now Sammy cried and cried
Because there was nowhere to hide.
He snuggled down into the hay,
but the farmer took it all away.

"Now just look at what we have here."
The farmer smiled from ear to ear.
"I believe our little stowaway
must have been playing in the hay."

And then everything went dark.

All Sammy could hear was his pounding heart.

When Sammy was put back in the light,

he saw everything was all right.

Across the yard, he saw his tree.

He hurried home quick as a bee.

He raced up in the big oak's cover
and came face-to-face with his mother.
"Now do you believe what I say
about naughty squirrels who roll in the hay?"

With that, she gave him a big hug,

and he knew he was safe and snug.

Sammy made a vow that day,

he would listen to what his mother had to say.

About the Author

Cristi Ropp has always dreamed of being a successful children's book author, and now she is proof that you are never too old to reach for the stars and watch your dreams come true.

CPSIA information can be obtained
at www.ICGtesting.com
Printed in the USA
BVHW021021080621
609012BV00009B/1963